THE REMARKABLE RESCUE OF
WARRAGUL WHALE

WORDS AND PICTURES
BY SIMON McLEAN

in collaboration with Carolina Häggström McLean

The waters of Humpback Bay were alive
with the thrashing and splashing of whales.

Warragul was the youngest and he sang as he dipped and dived:
"Wheeeeeeeooooooo, wheeeeeeeooooooo.
I'm a humpback whale from my head to my tail.
My home is the sea – where whales love to be."

The ocean was full of new discoveries for Warragul –
new places to go and new creatures to meet.

While Warragul explored, the big whales swam close by.
They sang special songs that rumbled through the waters,
teaching him the lessons of the sea.

"Learn from the ocean, be it fair or foul weathered,
Care for all creatures, be they fishy or feathered.
Swim with the tide, but beware of the sand,
For whales cannot live very long on dry land."

Warragul was splashing along listening to the songs of the whales,
when suddenly a penguin popped up in a panic.
"Help!" she spluttered. "A cranky old seal wants to make me its meal!"

"We'll see about that," said Warragul
as he ducked under the water.

"Stop that, old seal! How would you feel
if I chased you? – Now shoo!"

The seal dashed off and Warragul brought
the penguin back to the surface.

"You've saved me, you've saved me," puffed the penguin.
"I was not in the mood to become someone's food.
But now I'm so tired and sore, I'll never make it back to shore."

Warragul peered over the waves towards the land.
"I can take you," he bubbled.

"You can?" chirped the penguin hopefully.
"Of course," answered Warragul.

"A penguin is a penguin and a whale is a whale,
But a friend is a friend in calm, storm or gale."

So Warragul sped off towards the shore
with his grateful passenger.

The young whale swam on, coming closer to the land,
where the huge swells rose and crashed.

He surfed onto a wave and away they zoomed.
"Yippee!" cried the penguin gleefully.

But the wave suddenly dumped with a
W H U M M P P !
and the friends went
K A F L U M M P P !
onto the sand.

"Brrrkkk!" clucked the penguin.
"We're covered in foam,
but what a great way to get home."

But Warragul wasn't so happy.
"Oh no," he groaned. "This is no place for a whale.
Whales need to be free to dive and play in the sea."

"Don't worry, Warragul. I'll rescue you," cried the penguin.
She tried pushing the whale towards the water.
She pushed and pushed with all her might,
but Warragul didn't budge.
He was far too big for one small penguin.

Warragul was stranded.

"A whale needs to be free to dive and play in the sea," he mumbled tearfully.
The penguin wrapped her wings around Warragul.
"I won't leave you stuck," she promised.
"Remember . . . though I'm a small penguin and you're a big whale,
A friend is a friend in calm, storm or gale.
I won't give up," she whispered.

The little penguin jumped up.
"When the going gets hard,
call the penguin lifeguard," she cried.

And she let out a special penguin call:
"Crrkka, crrkka, brrkk, brrkk."

And penguins popped up everywhere!

"Penguins all, hear my call," squawked the little penguin.
"Warragul saved me when my future looked grim.
Now he's in trouble, let's try and help him."

The penguins charged down the beach . . .
took up their positions . . .
and when the little penguin gave the signal . . .

they pushed and pushed and heaved and huffed . . .

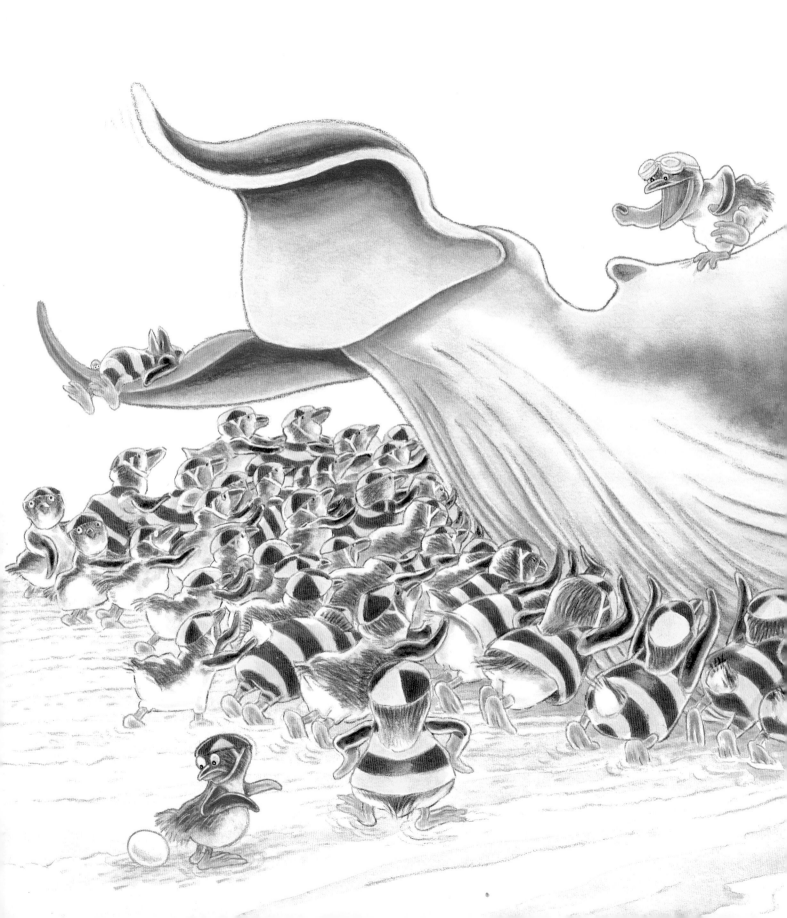

then finally... with one big heave from the penguins
and with one great flap of his tail...

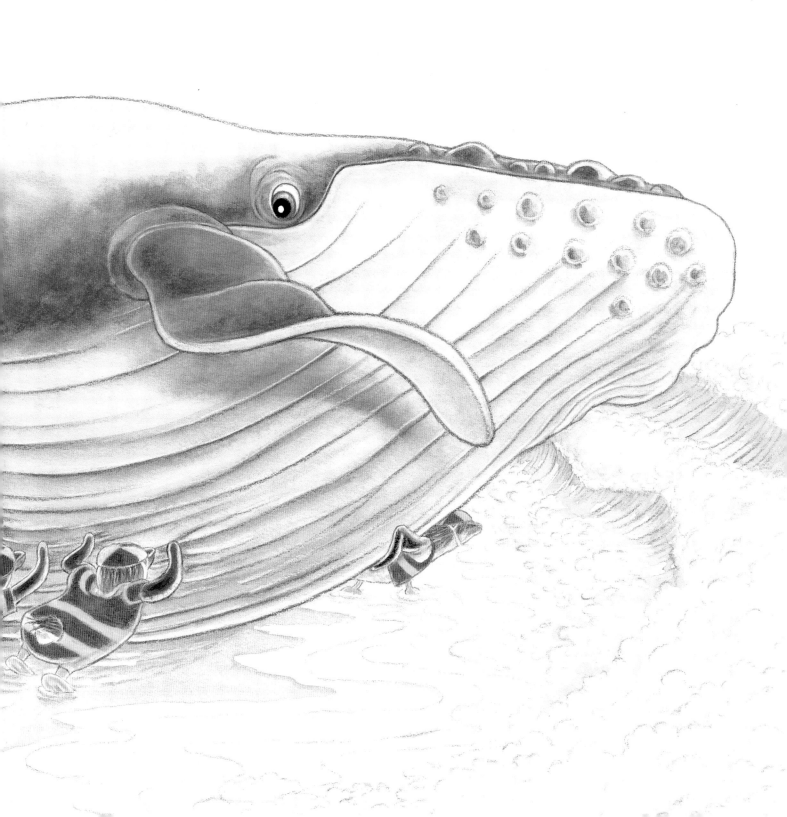

Warragul whooshed off the beach
and splashed into the water.

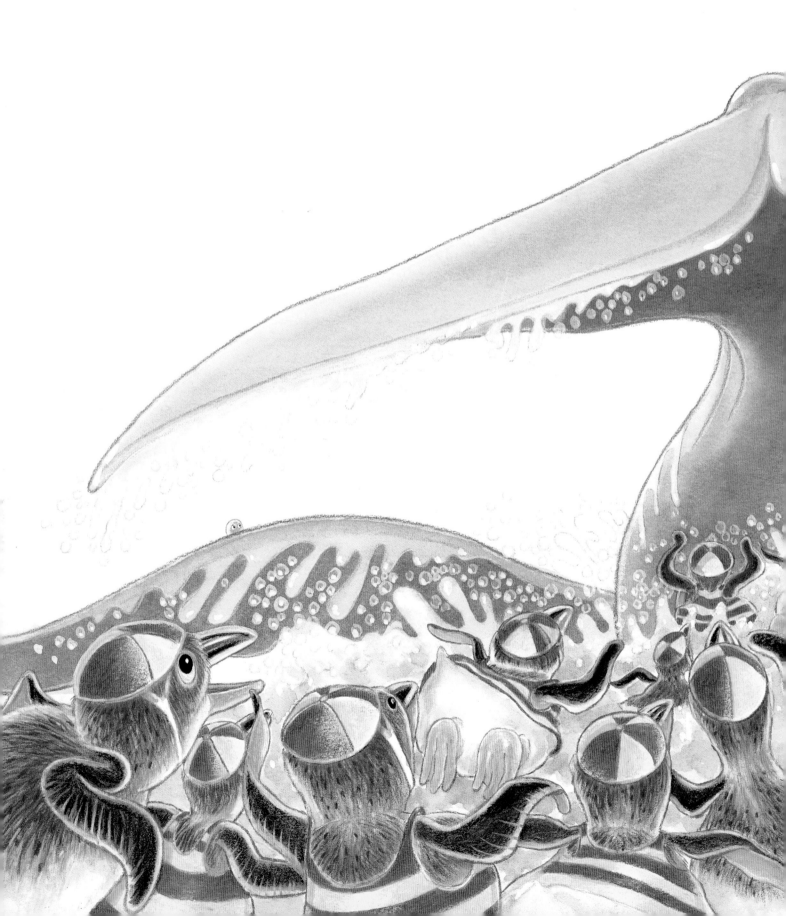

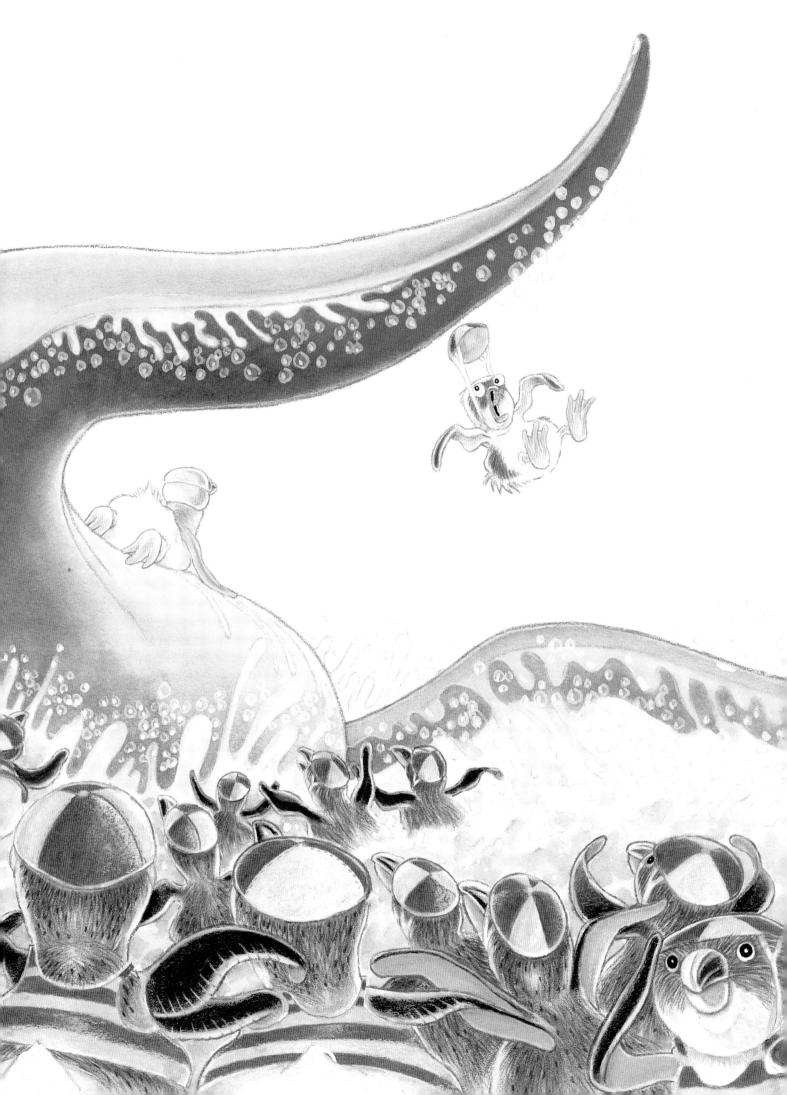

"Hurray," shouted the penguins.
"I'm free," shouted Warragul.
"Salt water feels better than dry land to me,
so from now on I think that I'll stay in the sea."

And he leapt over
the waves in joy.

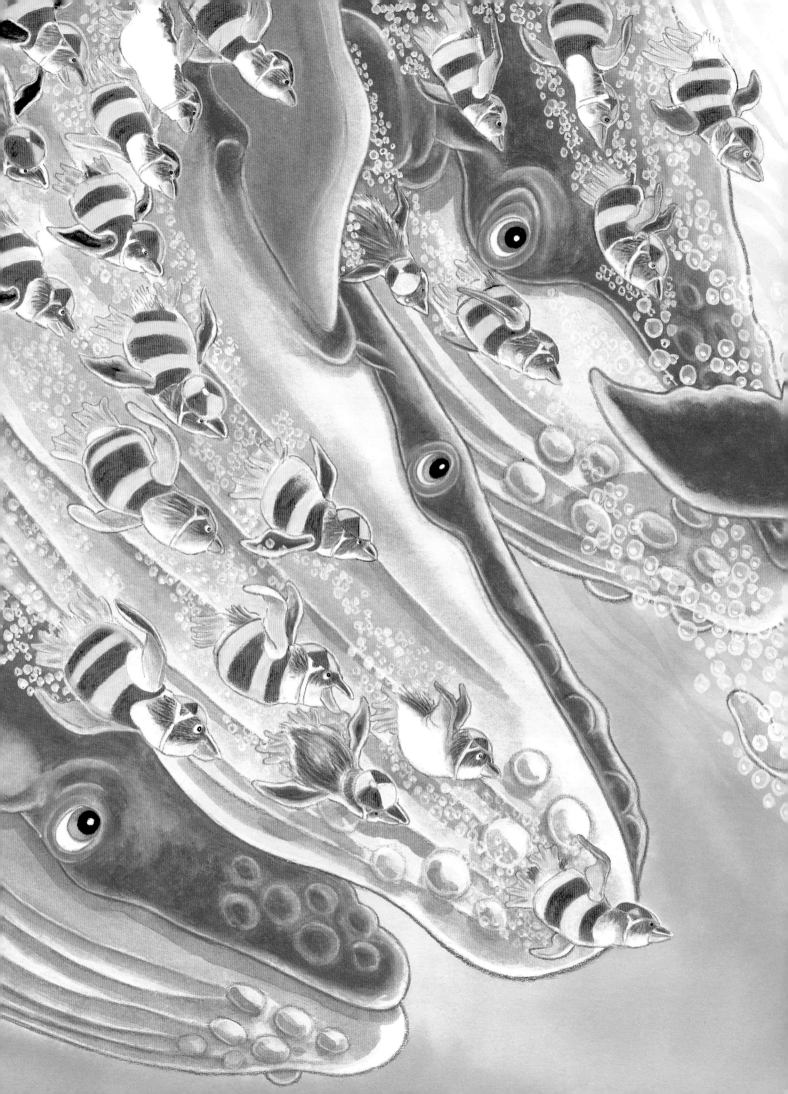

The penguins chirped and cheered,
  as the big whales gathered around Warragul.
   And their songs echoed through the ocean:
    "He's free, he's free, his home is the sea,
      for Warragul Whale it's the best place to be."

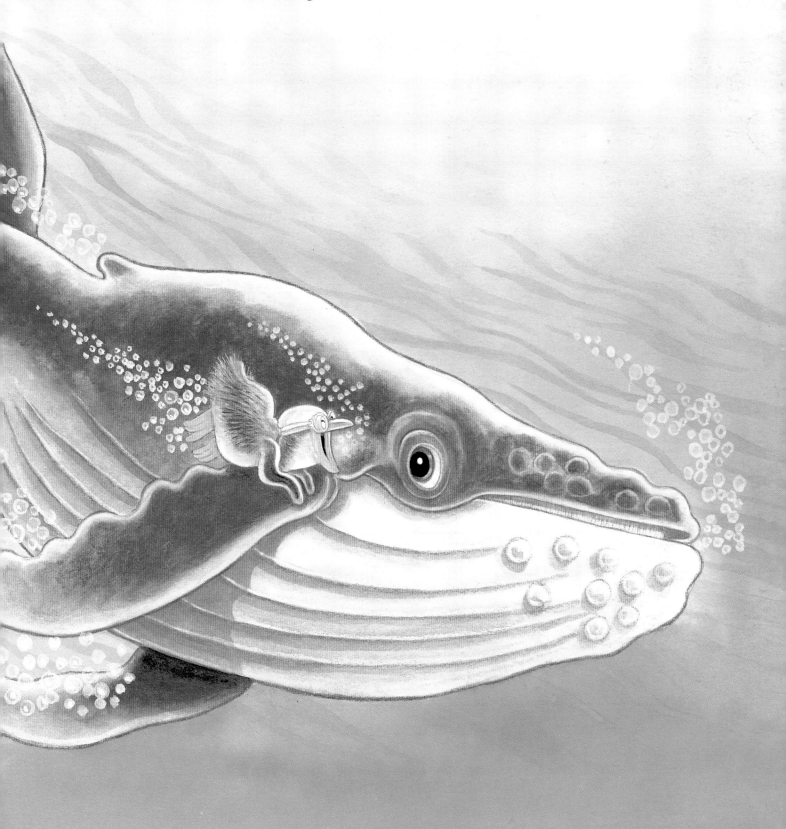

Yes, for Warragul, the sea
is the best place to be.

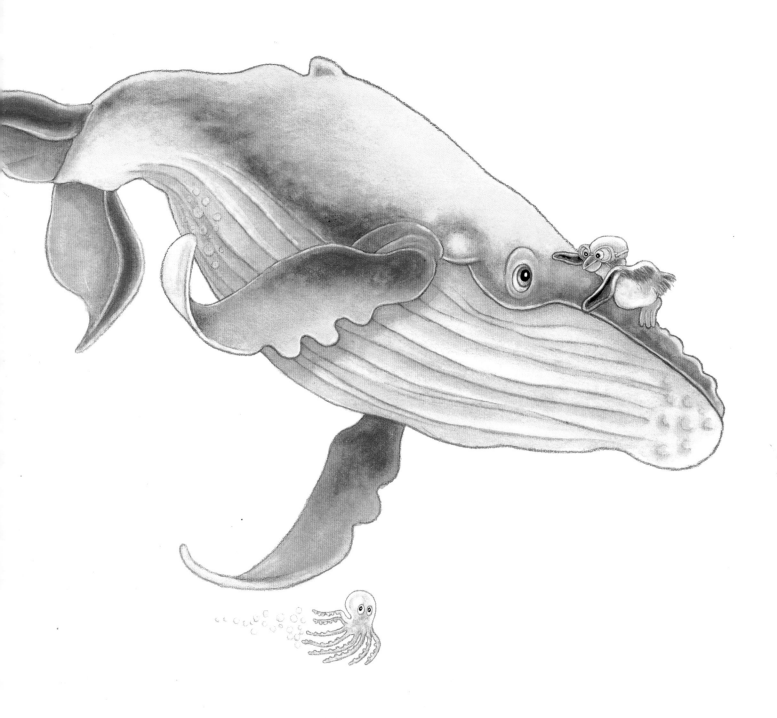